DAVID SUZUKI

BOMPA'S INSECT EXPEDITION

WITH **TANYA LLOYD KYI**   ILLUSTRATED BY **QIN LENG**

DAVID SUZUKI INSTITUTE

GREYSTONE KIDS

GREYSTONE BOOKS • VANCOUVER/BERKELEY/LONDON

Nakina and her twin brother, Kaoru, are going on a nature expedition with their grandpa.

Nakina fills her backpack with everything they might need.

Kaoru grabs his field journal.

When Bompa arrives,

they're ready!

"Where are we going?"
Nakina asks.

They can never guess where
Bompa will take them.

Sometimes they visit ponds in search of frogs' eggs. Sometimes they peer into tide pools at the beach. They imagine they're explorers, searching for discoveries.

And no matter what, they always find surprises.

Who knows what they'll find next?

Bompa shakes his head.

"We don't have much time today," he says, "so we're going on an expedition right here at home. We're going to search for...insects!"

The twins' eyes grow wide. They love insects! But...wait. They already know all about the creatures near their house.

"Bompa, I've drawn pictures of every single thing around here," Kaoru says.

Bompa heads outside, peeking into leaves and peering into flowers as he goes.

"Let's see what we find," he says. "You might be surprised."

Nakina follows him.

"Bompa, I know where to find insects.
There are always bees buzzing by the clover."

The three of them gather to watch
a fuzzy bumblebee gathering pollen.

"Bompa, are insects animals?" Nakina asks.

"Like walruses and iguanas and hammerhead
sharks?" Those are three of her favorites.

"Of course," Bompa says. "They all need the same things to survive: food, water, air, and safe spaces to live. And insects are a lot like you and me. They have brains to think and eyes to see."

"But they have six legs instead of two," Kaoru says.

Bompa nods. "And some of them have wings!"

He sounds like *he* wants six legs and wings too.

Just then, a dragonfly zooms past them.

"Imagine if we were insects!" Kaoru says.

"Our eyes could see up, down, and side to side, all at the same time," Bompa says.

"And we'd have shells," Nakina adds.

"That's right," Bompa says. "Instead of bones inside our bodies, we'd have exoskeletons to protect us. We could crash into walls without getting hurt. And if we were insects, we could dip and dive better than the best airplane pilots in the world."

Flying would be amazing. But Nakina knows about another creature that lives much closer to the ground.

"Bompa, I know where to find more insects," she calls.

Kaoru peers over her shoulder.
"Is a caterpillar an insect?" he wonders aloud.

Bompa smiles as if the twins have found treasure.

"Yes! Soon, that caterpillar will become a monarch butterfly," he says. "But first, it's going to gobble up milkweed. About two hundred times its own weight in leaves!"

That's a *lot* of leaves.

Kaoru's favorite lunch is salmon and rice. Nakina likes carrots.
And they both *love* ice cream.

What if they could eat two hundred times their own weight?
Life would be all about lunch!

"Why does it eat so much?" Nakina asks.

"It needs energy to build its chrysalis, the snug little home that keeps it safe while it transforms into a butterfly," Bompa says. "Imagine if you were going to grow wings, six legs, a new head and body . . . you'd certainly need extra snacks!"

"Bompa, I know where to find insects too,"
Kaoru says. "There's an ant nest around here!"

Bompa and Kaoru bound over and flatten
themselves on the ground to look.

When Nakina tries to join them, her heavy pack tugs her sideways.

It sways.

It slides.

And then ... SPLAT! She ends up flat.

Once they know she's okay, Kaoru and Bompa burst into giggles.

Even Nakina has to laugh.

Bompa glances again at the ants. "Imagine if you were an ant. You could carry a whole *stack* of backpacks."

Nakina's mouth drops open. She's surprised that insects are so strong!

"I've never sketched ant muscles before," Kaoru says, pulling out his journal.

"Why do they need to lift so much?" Nakina asks.

But as she watches, she notices something. "They're carrying food back to their nest!"

Hey! *Bzzzz!*

Nakina forgets all about ants.
Now she can only see mosquitoes.

"Bompa, I know where to find even more insects," she cries.
"And they're trying to eat us!"

She swats at another one.

"Bompa," Kaoru says, with a trace of mischief,
"what would happen if there were no mosquitoes?"

Bompa's eyebrows go up. Way up.

"Birds, bats, and frogs feed on mosquitoes. If there were no insects, many of those creatures would disappear," he says.

He points to some flowers. "Plants can't move around like we do. They need insects to carry pollen from one flower to the next. If there were no insects, the plants couldn't make seeds or fruit. Just imagine . . ."

"That doesn't sound good," Nakina admits.

"Not good at all!" Kaoru says.

Then another mosquito lands on Nakina.

She watches it for a moment before brushing it away.

"What if *we* disappeared?"
she wonders.

What would the world be like without humans?

Nakina thinks about the noisy cars, the garbage in parks, the chemicals sprayed on flowers and crops.

Without those things, the world would be full of fruits and flowers, birds and butterflies.

"If we were gone . . ." her brother says, looking at his feet.

Nakina sighs. "The other animals would be left alone. No one would even miss us."

"*What!?* I would miss you!"
Bompa says.

"Who would I take on expeditions?
Who would play games with me?
Who would find new ways to
surprise me every time I visit?"

Bompa gazes down at the twins.
"Humans are incredible creatures, too."

"And we can make things better!"
Nakina says.

"We all need insects, but I need you," Bompa says. He wraps Kaoru and Nakina in a giant Bompa-hug, the very best kind.

Then he stops, scratching his head. "You know what else I need? Food! Do we have any snacks?"

Yes! Nakina knew her pack would be useful.

"I have snacks, Bompa. Expedition snacks!"

Bompa grins. "See? What would I do without you, Nakina and Kaoru?"

Soon, Bompa, Kaoru, and Nakina
are picnicking on the grass.

"Nakina, what's that by your elbow?"
Kaoru points to a leaf at the edge
of the blanket. It's not a leaf at all!

"Good spotting, Kaoru. You've found a green lacewing!" Bompa says.

"Whoa!" Kaoru leans closer.

Nakina digs a magnifying glass from her pack so they can both get an up-close look.

"How did you even see it? It's perfectly hidden," she says.

Bompa nods. "It's an expert at hide-and-seek."

The lacewing stretches one leg toward Kaoru, almost as if it's offering a tiny high-five.

Bompa grabs an apple and sits back happily.

"Look!" Nakina grins. "Some of the other insects are joining us."

The twins don't mind the new arrivals. After all, insects are competitive eaters, champion weight lifters, and expert fliers. They're the world's most interesting picnic guests.

"We found so many creatures today," Kaoru says. "And we barely left home."

"Discoveries just outside our door!" Nakina agrees.

"What a surprise," Bompa says.

Nakina thinks she sees him wink at the lacewing. But that must be her imagination.

KAORU'S FIELD JOURNAL

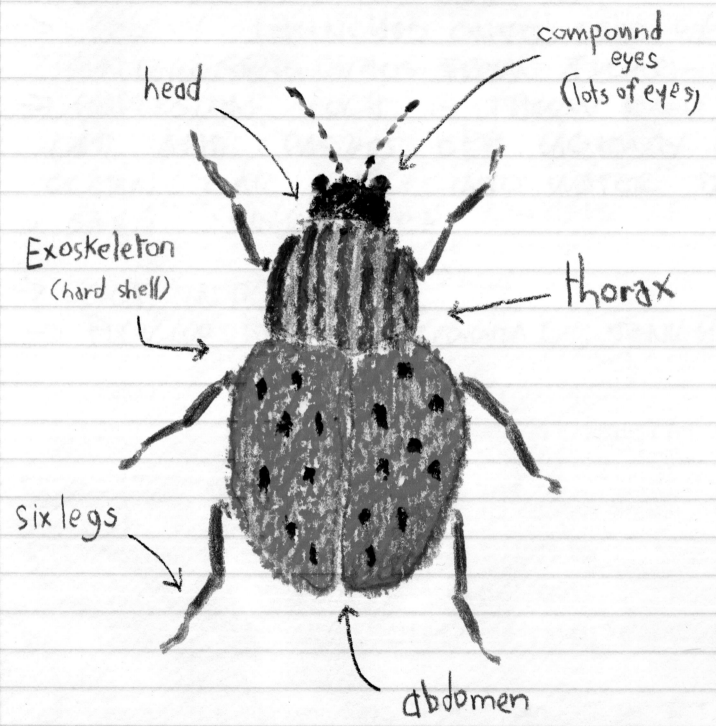

head

compound
eyes
(lots of eyes)

Exoskeleton
(hard shell)

thorax

Six legs

abdomen

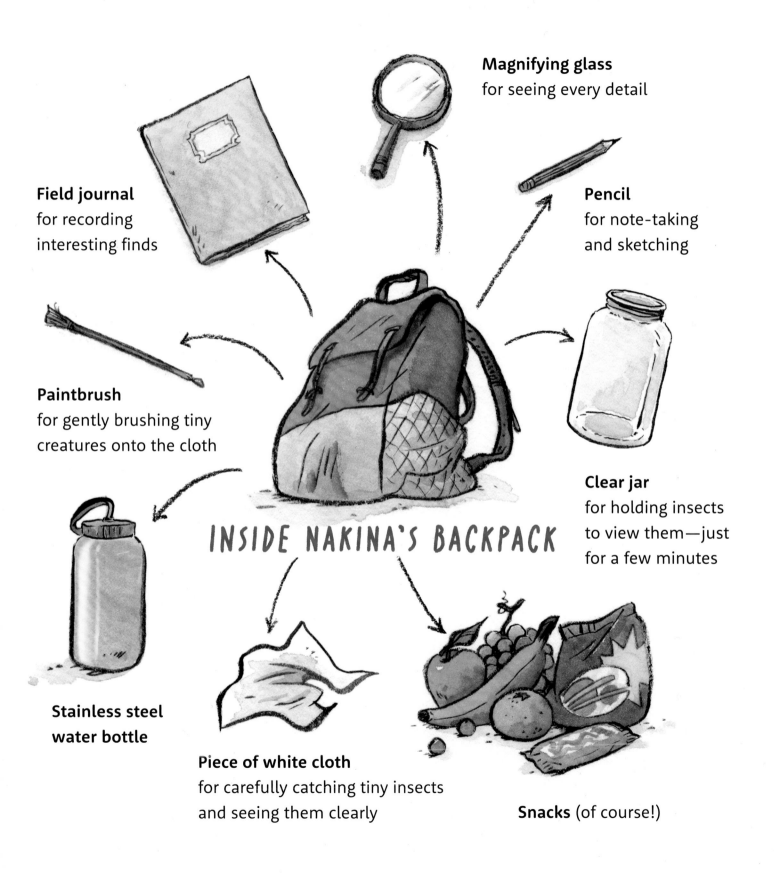

Magnifying glass
for seeing every detail

Field journal
for recording
interesting finds

Pencil
for note-taking
and sketching

Paintbrush
for gently brushing tiny
creatures onto the cloth

Clear jar
for holding insects
to view them—just
for a few minutes

INSIDE NAKINA'S BACKPACK

**Stainless steel
water bottle**

Piece of white cloth
for carefully catching tiny insects
and seeing them clearly

Snacks (of course!)

MORE AMAZING INSECT FACTS

The creatures in these pages really are some of the most amazing on Earth.

You already know some of them from your neighborhood: the ants that march past on the sidewalk, the bees that make you honey, and the butterflies that capture your attention with their vibrant wings.

Here are a few more of Bompa's favorites.

- **Fruit flies.** They're tiny, but they're a lot like us. They have many of the same genes. That's why scientists like Bompa love to study them. In fact, scientists have been studying fruit flies for more than a hundred years!

- **Dragonflies.** Backwards, forwards, side to side—these insects can zoom in any direction. They can hover in place or fly upside down. Dragonflies have been whizzing around the world since the time of the dinosaurs.

- **Click beetles.** They have a notch on their thorax that makes a loud CLICK and flips the beetle into the air, to scare away predators. (The ability to flip is also helpful when click beetles land on their backs!)

- **Mayflies.** After they hatch, most mayflies live only a day or two. When Bompa was a little boy, there were so many mayflies, they'd cover whole roads and houses. Today, many of them have been killed by pollution and pesticides (poisons that kill insects). That's part of the reason Bompa works so hard to teach people to appreciate insects and protect them.

YOU CAN HELP INSECTS THRIVE

Nakina and Kaoru love insects. And the world needs insects. These tiny creatures feed fish, frogs, bats, birds, and even bears. They pollinate flowers so new fruits grow. They snack on rotten things and help keep the forests clean.

But insects are in trouble, and they need our help. Could you be an insect hero?

Here are some things you can do...

- **Go green.** Whenever you can, choose organic fruits and vegetables grown without pesticides. You'll be saving insects and eating healthy at the same time.

- **Plant a flower.** At the local garden shop, ask what kinds of flowers the insects in your neighborhood need. Then plant a seed on your balcony or in your yard.

- **Get messy.** Leave some sticks and leaves on your lawn for the winter, or let a few plants go wild on your windowsill. You'll be helping insects find cozy homes.

- **Start a bug club.** Hunt for insects! Take pictures, collect facts, and tell your friends why tiny creatures are so important.

WHAT OTHER INSECTS CAN YOU FIND?

Look through these pages again.
How many different insects can you find
in the twins' neighborhood?
Can you find...

Entomologist
(en-tuh-MOL-uh-jist)

A scientist who
studies insects.

- something that flies?

- something with spots?

- something with big eyes?

- something that hops?

Bompa, Nakina, and Kaoru love *all* insects, whether they buzz or sting, leap through the air or fly loop the loops. And they're constantly discovering new insect facts.

There are about a million different species of insects in the world ... and those are just the ones that scientists have named. There are probably millions of others waiting to be discovered. Maybe you'll discover your own favorites one day soon!

DAVID SUZUKI is an internationally renowned scientist and environmentalist who has made it his life's work to help humanity understand, appreciate, respect, and protect nature. Suzuki is a Companion to the Order of Canada and a recipient of UNESCO's Kalinga Prize for the Popularization of Science, the 2009 Right Livelihood Award, and UNEP's Global 500 Award. For decades, he hosted the popular CBC television program *The Nature of Things*. He is the co-founder of the David Suzuki Foundation and the author of more than fifty books. He lives in Vancouver, BC, and is a father of five and grandfather to ten, including twins Nakina and Kaoru.

TANYA LLOYD KYI is the award-winning author of more than thirty books for children and young adults. Her most recent books include *What Will I Discover?*; *Our Green City*; *Better Connected* (written with her daughter, Julia Kyi); and *The Best Way to Get Your Way*. Tanya lives in Vancouver, BC, where she teaches for the University of British Columbia's School of Creative Writing.

QIN LENG is a visual development artist and an illustrator and author of children's books. Throughout her career, she has illustrated picture books, magazines, and book covers with publishers around the world. Recent books include *I Am Small*, her author-illustrator debut, *A Day for Sandcastles* written by JonArno Lawson, and *Clover* written by Nadine Robert which received the Governor General Literary Award for best picture book. She lives in Toronto with her husband and her son. You can find more about her work at www.qinillustrations.com.

Text copyright © 2023 by David Suzuki and Tanya Lloyd Kyi
Illustrations copyright © 2023 by Qin Leng

23 24 25 26 27 5 4 3 2 1

Greystone Kids / Greystone Books Ltd.
greystonebooks.com

David Suzuki Institute
davidsuzukiinstitute.org

Cataloguing data available from Library and Archives Canada
ISBN 978-1-77164-882-0 (cloth)
ISBN 978-1-77164-883-7 (epub)

Editing by Kallie George
Copy editing by Dawn Loewen
Proofreading by Becky Noelle
Jacket and interior design by Sara Gillingham Studio

The illustrations in this book were rendered in ink and watercolor.

Printed and bound in China on FSC® certified paper at Shenzhen Reliance Printing.
The FSC® label means that materials used for the product have been responsibly sourced.

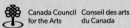

Greystone Books gratefully acknowledges the xʷməθkʷəy̓əm (Musqueam),
Sk̲wx̲wú7mesh (Squamish), and səlílwətaɬ (Tsleil-Waututh) peoples on
whose land our Vancouver head office is located.

The David Suzuki Institute is a companion organization to the David Suzuki Foundation, with a focus on promoting
and publishing on important environmental issues in partnership with Greystone Books.

We invite you to support the activities of the Institute. For more information, please contact us at:

David Suzuki Institute
219 – 2211 West 4th Avenue
Vancouver, BC, Canada V6K 4S2
info@davidsuzukiinstitute.org
604-742-2899
davidsuzukiinstitute.org

Cheques can be made payable to The David Suzuki Institute.